SiTTiNG DucK

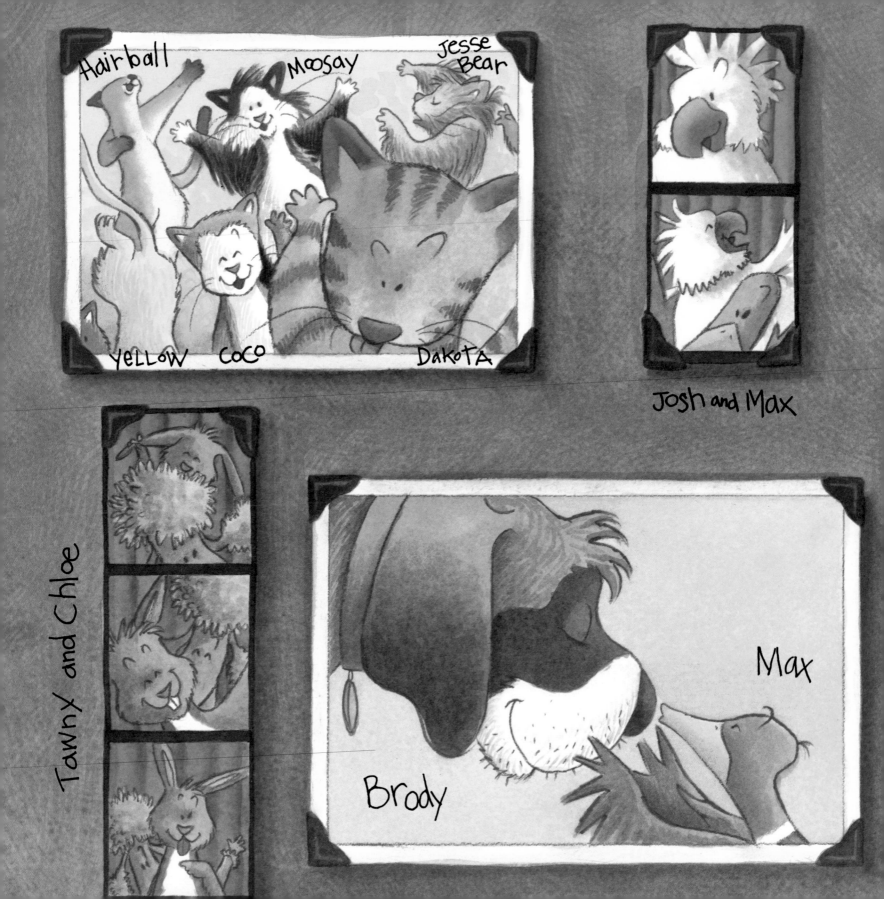

For my older sister, Pam, who was my babysitter.
And for my nieces, Kathy, Karen, Kris,
and Josi, whom I watched over.
We made each other crazy. I laugh about it still.

And a special thank-you to Caleb and Corina, who gave this book its title.

ISBN 978-0-545-43901-5

Copyright © 2010 by Jackie Urbanovic. All rights reserved.
Published by Scholastic Inc., 557 Broadway, New York, NY 10012, by arrangement with
HarperCollins Children's Books, a division of HarperCollins Publishers. SCHOLASTIC
and associated logos are trademarks and/or registered trademarks of Scholastic Inc.

12 11 10 9 8 7 6 5 4 3 2 1   12 13 14 15 16 17/0

Printed in the U.S.A.   76

This edition first printing, January 2012

Typography by Rachel Zegar

SITTING DUCK

Jackie Urbanovic

SCHOLASTIC INC.
New York Toronto London Auckland
Sydney Mexico City New Delhi Hong Kong

"Babysitting is easy!" said Brody. "When Anabel gets here, we'll all play together. Our only job will be to keep her out of trouble."

"Sure," said Max. "How much trouble could a puppy get into, anyway?"

"Babysitting, huh?" said Chloe. "It sounds like a LOT of trouble to me."

"I suggest we make a run for it. Everyone else is going," said Dakota.

"Out the back door, QUICK!" yelled Bebe.

"She's at the front door already!"

"UNCLE BRODY!"
said Anabel.

"Anabel, this is your Uncle Max and Uncle Dov," said Brody.

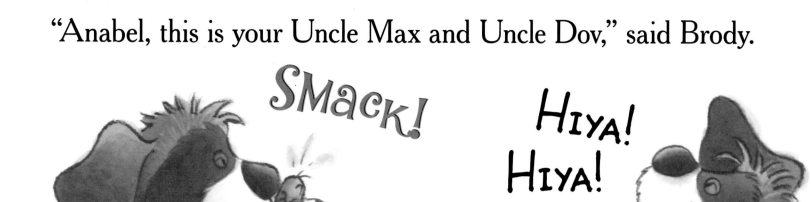

SMACK!

HIYA! HIYA!

"LET'S PLAY!"

shouted Anabel.

They played dress up . . .

and silly faces . . .

and chef . . .

and ball. . . .

"ENOUGH!" yelled Brody.

"Someone needs a nap!" said Brody.

"Let's play hide 'n' seek,"
said Anabel.

I'VE HAD ENOUGH!
SEE YOU LATER, GUYS.

Brody sat Anabel down for a story and a nap. "Does this mean we aren't going to play hide 'n' seek?" asked Anabel.

"Just listen and—yawn—relax," said Brody.
So Anabel listened and Brody, well, relaxed.

UNCLE
MAXIE!

"I thought you were napping!"
said Max.

"Uncle Brody's napping. I want
to go outside!" said Anabel.

"Outside?" Max considered the idea. "Well, I did want to get some outdoor shots . . . and how much trouble could a puppy get into, anyway?"

"YIPPPPEEEEEEEE!"

yelled Anabel.

"SHHHHHHHHH!"
said Max.

"What would you like to
do?" asked Max. "Swing?"
"EEK!" said Anabel.

"Swim?" suggested Max.
"I don't think so . . ." said Anabel.

"Bounce?" asked Max.
"YES, BOUNCE!" said Anabel.
"Okay, then! Ready, set, GO!" said Max.

"CLICK"

They bounced!
They flew!

Up and down.
Higher and higher.

Until Max realized he was bouncing alone.

"Anabel?"   "Anabel?"

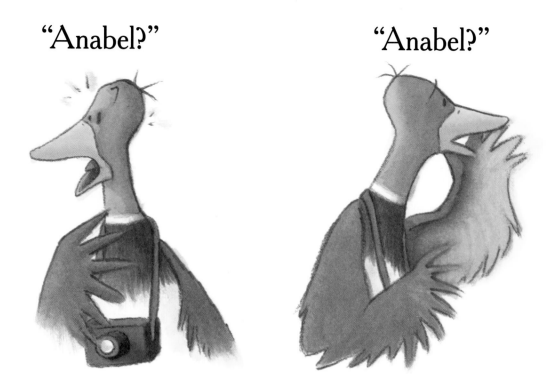

"ANABEL!
WHERE ARE YOU!?" shouted Max.

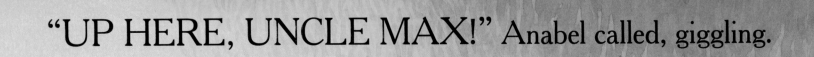

"UP HERE, UNCLE MAX!" Anabel called, giggling.

"DON'T MOVE, ANABEL! NOT ONE INCH! I'M GOING TO GET HELP!" yelled Max.

Max returned with Brody and an idea.
"I'll pull down on the branch until you slide off," Max explained.
"Okay, Uncle Max," said Anabel.
"Be careful now," warned Brody.

"GRAB MY
LEGS, BRODY!"
yelled Max.
"PULL!"

"Oops!"

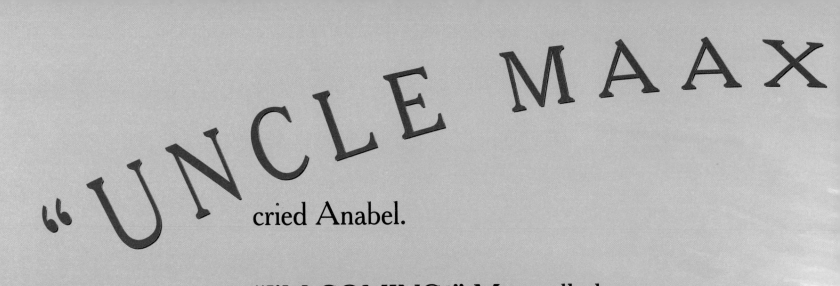

"UNCLE MAAX

cried Anabel.

"I'M COMING!" Max called,
while Brody pushed the trampoline
toward Anabel to cushion her fall.

"AIM FOR THE TRAMP!!" yelled Brody.
And she did. With a little help.

WHOOMP!

Anabel bounced to safety along with—*BOING*—her—*BOING*—rescuers—*BOING, BOING!*

"Anabel," gasped Max. "Are you all right?"
"That was FUN, Uncle Max! Let's do it again!" said Anabel.

At six p.m. Irene returned home.
"Okay, I can take Anabel home now.
Where is she?"
"Napping," said Moosay.
"So it went well?" asked Irene.
"FINE!" said Scrappy.
"No problem," said Chloe.

"Really," said Tawny.
"How much trouble could a
puppy get into, anyway?"